The Drug Awareness Library

Danger:
MARIJUANA

Ruth Chier

The Rosen Publishing Group's
PowerKids Press
New York

Published in 1996 by The Rosen Publishing Group, Inc.
29 East 21st Street, New York, NY 10010

First Edition

Book design: Erin McKenna

Photo credits: Cover by Michael Brandt; p. 7 by Kathleen McClancy; p. 12 by Guillermina DeFerrari; p. 16 © Caroline Wood/International Stock; p. 18 © Dusty Willison/International Stock; all other photos by Sarah Friedman.

Chier, Ruth.
    Danger: marijuana / Ruth Chier
        p.   cm. — (The Drug awareness library)
    Includes index.
    Summary: Discusses the effects of marijuana on humans and the value of avoiding its use.
    ISBN 0-8239-2335-5
    1. Marijuana—Juvenile literature. 2. Drug abuse—Juvenile literature. 3. Substance abuse—Prevention—Juvenile literature. 4. Marijuana—Psychological aspects—Juvenile literature. 5. Marijuana—Physiological effect—Juvenile literature. [1. Marijuana. 2. Drug abuse.] I. Title. II. Series.
HV5822.M3C48 1996
362.29'5—dc20   95-50791
                                                                      CIP
                                                                       AC

Manufactured in the United States of America

Contents

Bad Drugs and Good Drugs

Drugs affect how you feel and think and act. Some drugs help your body. These drugs, called medicines, are usually given to you by your parent or a doctor. Medicine helps you get well if you are sick.

Other drugs hurt your body. They are usually **illegal** (il-LEE-gul). Illegal drugs are dangerous. Sometimes people use illegal drugs anyway. **Marijuana** (mare-i-WA-na) is one kind of illegal drug.

◀ Medicine is a drug. It can help you get well when you are sick.

What Is Marijuana?

Marijuana comes from a plant called *Cannabis sativa.* The strong fibers of the marijuana plant, also called hemp, have been used for hundreds of years to make cloth, paper, and rope.

Marijuana is grown in many places around the world. Some people call marijuana "maryjane," "pot," "grass," or "weed."

It is against the law to grow marijuana. ▶

How Is Marijuana Used?

The leaves of the marijuana plant are dried and then rolled in paper and smoked. This is called a "joint" or a "reefer." Marijuana can also be smoked in a certain kind of pipe.

When someone inhales the smoke, it goes through the lungs and into the **bloodstream** (BLUD-streem). Then it reaches the brain. It hurts your body along the way.

Marijuana can also be eaten. Sometimes it is baked in foods like brownies.

◀ Marijuana can be eaten, but it is usually smoked like a cigarette or in a certain kind of pipe.

9

The Effects of Marijuana

When a person uses marijuana, he gets "**high**" (HY) or "**stoned**" (STONED). It makes him act silly and laugh a lot. It also makes him feel very hungry.

Some people think it is fun to use marijuana. They do not realize that using marijuana hurts them.

When a person is high, he or she may act silly or laugh a lot. ▶

Marijuana Hurts You

Marijuana changes the way your body works. At first it makes you feel high. It slows down your thinking and breathing. It can make your hands and feet very cold and make you feel dizzy. It can make your heart beat fast and your eyes turn red.

The feeling of being high lasts only a little while. Then you feel tired, sad, and sometimes even sick to your stomach.

◀ Using marijuana can make you feel dizzy or sick to your stomach.

Marijuana Changes You

You probably like to watch TV or play with your friends or read. If you use marijuana, you might laugh and act silly for a little while.

But when the marijuana wears off, you won't want to play baseball or ride your bike or see your friends. You'll forget that you have homework or that your dad said he would take you to the movies. All you'll want to do is use more marijuana.

Using marijuana makes you less interested in doing anything else. ▶

Why People Use Marijuana

Sometimes people use marijuana because they think it is fun or exciting, or it makes them feel grown-up. Some people use it because their friends do.

Some people use it to run away from problems in their lives. When they are high, they may forget their problems. But using marijuana really makes a person have more problems.

◀ People don't need to get high to have fun.

What Is Addiction?

When a person uses a drug for a long time, he can become **addicted** (a-DIK-ted) to it, or "hooked." Having an addiction means that you are **dependent** (dee-PEN-dent) on a drug. You can't stop using the drug. You feel sick without it.

People who are addicted to a drug are called addicts. Addicts feel that they need the drug the same way that other people need food, water, and sleep.

Addicts feel that they need drugs the way that most people need food. ▶

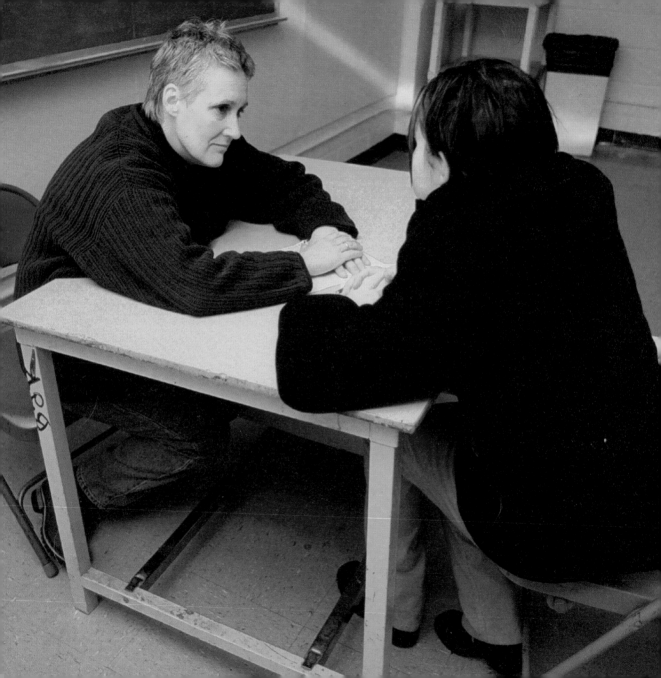

Marijuana and Your Friends

You may know someone who uses marijuana, maybe even one of your friends. This friend might ask you to try it. He might say that you're not cool if you don't try it. Or he might say that you are scared. Nobody can make you do something you don't want to do. All you have to say if someone offers you marijuana is, "No, thanks. I don't do drugs."

◀ Teenagers often talk to adults about drugs and what to say to friends who use them. You can too.

Ending Addiction

Addicts are not bad people. They may not understand that they are hurting themselves. And they may not know how to stop.

There are many places addicts can go for help. They can talk to a parent, a teacher, or a minister. They can also call a drug hotline, and someone will talk to them about getting help.

It is not easy to recover from an addiction, but it is possible.

Glossary

addicted (a-DIK-ted) When a person can't control his or her use of a drug.

bloodstream (BLUD-streem) The way blood flows through your body.

dependent (dee-PEN-dent) Relying on a drug to feel good.

high (HI) Using drugs to change the way you think or feel.

illegal (il-LEE-gul) Against the law.

marijuana (mare-i-WA-na) Drug that slows down a person's body and makes him or her see things that aren't there.

stoned (STONED) The feeling a person can have when using a drug.

Index

24